BURY MY HEART UNDER THE MARTIAN SKY

AND OTHER POEMS

JUAN MANUEL PÉREZ

This is a work of fiction. All of the characters, organizations, and events portrayed are either products of the author's imagination or used fictitiously.

BURY MY HEART UNDER THE MARTIAN SKY

Text Copyright © 2026 by Juan Manuel Pérez

All rights reserved. No part of this book may be reproduced in any form or by any electronic or mechanical means, including information storage and retrieval systems, without written permission from the author and publisher, except for the use of brief quotations in a book review.

Edited by Holly Lyn Walrath.

Cover art by Kolega Soberanis.

Cover Design by Holly Lyn Walrath.

The "chupacabra dog" in the cover border is inspired by the colima statues of Mesoamerica.

Published by Interstellar Flight Press, Houston, Texas.

www.interstellarflightpress.com

ISBN (Print): 978-1-953736-57-4

ISBN (EBook): 978-1-953736-56-7

First Edition: 2026

PRAISE FOR JUAN MANUEL PÉREZ

"Weaving futurist horizons with mythical histories, while marrying the grim with the wonderous, *Bury My Heart Under the Martian Sky* is a collection that will stand the test of time."

—PEDRO INIGUEZ, BRAM STOKER AND ELGIN AWARD-WINNING AUTHOR OF *MEXICANS ON THE MOON: SPECULATIVE POETRY FROM A POSSIBLE FUTURE*

"*Bury My Heart Under the Martian Sky* is a chapbook collection of things alien on many levels. At times dark, otherworldly, and humorous, the poems are an offshoot of Pérez's Mexican American/indigenous cultural background. Autobiographical at times, there be Chupacabras, Aztec historical references, mermaloids, the truth about cats, and other mythic allusions. This is a good read all around, and worthy of the poet's best work."

—G. O. CLARK, AUTHOR OF *TOMBSTONES: SELECTED HORROR POEMS*

"*Bury My Heart Under the Martian Sky* is a series of haiku 'crowns,' collections of haiku that work as a single poem, on fantastical and poignant topics. Pérez tackles both inner and outer aspects of horror, science fiction, and maybe, just maybe, science reality. Like any good haiku, these 'crowns' are cause for meditation and discussion. Who gets to go into space and why? What happens when the colonized become the colonizers? And merfolk, well, how do they see our intrusions into what they would see as their 'lands'? Not all the poems are as serious; there is fun and fantasy, too; still, Pérez finds room for rumination on the more serious ideas of space travel and perhaps colonization, and oh, yes, what to expect when the gods of the Aztecs return 'As if they ever left...'"

—DENISE DUMARS, AUTHOR OF *CAJUNS IN SPACE* AND *MARS MAUNDERING.*

"*Bury My Heart Under The Martian Sky* is a mesmerizing journey into the realms of the speculative, where the dance of words meets the tapestry of the universe. As the Poet Laureate of Corpus Christi, Texas, Pérez brings forth a unique voice that resonates with the heartbeat of his indigenous heritage. In this scifaiku odyssey, Pérez weaves a poetic spell that stretches from the enigmatic depths of the ocean, where mermaloids sing lullabies, to the ancient landscapes of South America visited by extraterrestrial beings. Each poem is an extraordinary example of science fiction haiku poetry at its finest, blending the familiar with the fantastic, inviting readers to explore the uncharted territories of imagination."

—WENDY VAN CAMP, ANAHEIM'S POET LAUREATE EMERITA AND AUTHOR OF *THE PLANETS*

CONTENTS

What Dogs Know About Cats, Part I	1
What Dogs Know About Cats, Part II	2
What Dogs Know About Cats, Part III	3
El Monstro de Mejico/The Monster of Mexico	4
At the Temple of the Snake	5
The Other People	6
This Blue World	7
Me by the Sea	8
The Mermaloids' Lament	9
Bone Necklace	10
October Candy	11
The Devil in the Woods: The Warning	12
The Devil in the Woods: He Speaks	13
Awoken	14
The Man Lost Between Forever and Ever	15
The Future Is Nigh	16
The Vast Green Ocean of the Late 21st Century	17
The Machine that Didn't Know	18
As Old as Stars	19
Space Man's Lament	21
Citlaltemini	23
Coyolxāuhqui 3000	25
Mexico City, 2101 AD	27
Carnivorous Indigenous	29
The Visit	30
Godzilla at the Pow Wow	31
the jettisoned	32
Red Eyes on Rockets	33
A Place Among Skies	34
Bury My Heart Under the Martian Sky	36

Author's Note	37
About the Author	45
About the Cover Artist	49
Acknowledgments	51
Interstellar Flight Press	53

What Dogs Know About Cats, Part I

cats are finicky
find someone that doesn't know
someone from this world

at the master's door
gazing to see who it is
greeting like old friends

master talks to them
more than he talks to his kind
odd for the humans

they ask for special
the master always complies
ice box full of it

routine sacrifice
he will give and give again
what he calls a meal

the cats stay happy
so they return when hungry
at least once a week

as for the special
his name was Bob or something
master disliked him

What Dogs Know About Cats, Part II

Cats are destroyers
find something they haven't touched
since the beginning

we've leaned into peace
break from perpetual war
calm, with watchful eyes

the face of the Sphinx
hides the forgotten story
a war nearly won

my kind almost gone
if not for our new masters
balanced the power

his face now the Sphinx's
yet with no true hold on cats
just long arrangements

although man now rules
cats will surely persevere
end longstanding peace

even if man fails
master will be kept alive
he feeds them mankind

What Dogs Know About Cats, Part III

cats are liquidy
find a place they can't get in
you will be lying

dogs know the secret
that which baffles master's kind
not really magic

cats are not from here
forgotten place among stars
wish they would return

cats know that we know
they will kill to keep it hid
ask master for me

those that come weekly
to eat master's sacrifice
report to others

liquid are thoughts too
for I have spoken this truth
they will find me out

someday they will come
I will be those cold pieces
casualty of war

El Monstro de Mejico/The Monster of Mexico

state of Coahuila
goat pens of Piedras Negras
old farm in the woods

a herdsman still lives
if, in fact, that is living
scared of his shadow

sometimes when he's drunk
you might hear him scream out loud
a fear from his past

then, in a whisper
as if to catch his last breath
you might hear him speak

of a deep, dark night
that he relives every day
while wasting away

fractions of the tale
of the loss of his left eye
unlucky friends

so much more went wrong
when hell came to men and goats
el chupacabras

At the Temple of the Snake

there are some whispers
pyramids under the sea
not the ones we knew

high knowledge of snakes
once reached beyond these dry lands
far before this time

once they were the gods
now they're hunted by a God
a few became less

there are some whispers
pyramids under the sea
not the ones we knew

placed in that garden
to see if man would return
worship of serpents

a few will tell you
where many believe it not
man, the little snake

there are some whispers
pyramids under the sea
not the ones we knew

The Other People

there are people there
in the deepest part of blue
watching and waiting

for whom and for when
that still remains the unknown
they refuse to say

but they watch and wait
as the people of the land
go about their way

there are people there
in the deepest part of blue
watching and waiting

they say that humans
once came from the vast oceans
but he soon forgot

now on a fast track
consuming the world he knows
looming combustion

there are people there
in the deepest part of blue
watching and waiting

This Blue World

mermaloid greetings
when man arrived on this world
leaving theirs behind

happy to be saved
that was mankind's beginning
life on makeshift boats

yet, it was not long
before his true intention
man was made for war

it is within him
this dreadful lust for bloodshed
this space transient

the sea people fled
deeper into the oceans
cursing all mankind

salting the blue world
drying all that man can touch
until he's no more

like he salts the world
to rid our cousins, the snails
one day beg for water

Me by the Sea

by the sea is me
stumped by a sweet siren's song
she perplexes me

by the sea is me
I had been warned of this, yet
she perplexes me

by the sea is me
bewildered by her beauty
she perplexes me

by the sea is me
she beckons to come to her
she perplexes me

by the sea is me
falling to her blissful kiss
she perplexes me

by the sea is me
heavy her grip on my neck
she perplexes me

falling for the sea
hoping you remember this . . .
she perplexes me

The Mermaloids' Lament

from oceans we came
when dry land was yet to be
when legs were fable

then we crawled on out
evolving from fins to limbs
taking steps away

before history
before the reed met the clay
when thoughts said it all

then to quill and ink
to write salty tales of old
of time out of place

forgot our purpose
we, descendants from the drink
all near washed away

now to screens and text
far from the call of the deep
far from once we were

war, we learned it well
cutting limbs away for peace
crawling back to sea

Bone Necklace

made a fine necklace
from the mermaid bones I found
where oceans once laid

seemed to call to me
maybe I imagined it
either way was real

when I wear the bones
I smell the oceans that were
under bluest skies

when I wear the bones
I swim through the old currents
coolness of the flow

when I wear the bones
I talk to all the sea life
whose names time forgot

when I wear the bones
I see all that flew above
listen to their splash

this made me wonder
if man ever existed
left no bones behind

October Candy

always delicious
caramel-coated secrets
filling head to toe

every known desire
into every shape of joy
pleasure without end

for one complete year
all the lust you could handle
for all your reasons

happy with your luck
you named the part, it was played
never asking why

shifting every mood
whatever flavor you liked
blonds, brunettes, redheads

as a year draws near
probably don't remember
October promise

she is still a witch
signed a contract with your blood
one year for your soul

The Devil in the Woods: The Warning

found what you looked for
it wasn't that difficult
path within the woods

you had been forewarned
don't look for him among pines
darkness masked as peace

the signs were all there
the right books had all declared
this was the wrong way

charm so deceiving
he is whatever you want
behold your madness

o' grand mask maker
speaker of beautiful lies
his control is whole

escape, there is none
your thoughts are no longer yours
your body as well

for he who warned you
is he who takes you himself
an alluring net

The Devil in the Woods: He Speaks

the things I will do
beyond your comprehension
pain and joy as one

you freely agreed
when I told you to stay away
entrance wide open

your body will do
I will devour your flesh
discard you when done

writhe in my essence
profound ecstasy and pain
nothing will compare

deep fornication
climax of flesh, mind, and soul
become one with me

the price of my love
precious seconds you will play
forever my slave

enjoy it, sweet servant
what follows, you will not like
eternal burning

Awoken

middle of the night
sound of metal in a tub
was I still dreaming?

so fresh of a sound
so alive with urgency
so sharp in my ears

turning on some lights
for whom was the message for
great interruption

everything normal
nothing seems out of its place
can't yet find a cause

what did it all mean?
was it something from the dream?
or straight from out here?

maybe dream itself
something it wanted to say
end I need not see

but what was that dream?
I can't even remember
here's to your success

The Man Lost Between Forever and Ever

a lost man to time
between thin layers of breath
there is no escape

everyone in sight
yet no one still to talk to
ears and eyes stitched tight

screaming at the walls
that do not speak nor they fall
like a spirit world

touch berths no feeling
the hungry do not hunger
desires dwindle

tried to end it all
death does not dwell in this place
all attempts have failed

astray with despair
painted with loud, frozen screams
here, the lost are lodged

there is no escape
between thin layers of breath
a lost man to time

The Future Is Nigh

air, air, everywhere
none of it of any worth
what we've done to earth

we've killed all the trees
planted metal-concrete seeds
land-scraped properties

we've killed all the bees
from fear of sting or disease
did as we damned pleased

air, air, everywhere
none of it of any worth
what we've done to earth

why, how can it be
abused the land, dried the sea
time to pay the fee

mankind, you and me
we've killed this world, don't you see
soon we have to flee

air, air, everywhere
none of it of any worth
what we've done to earth

The Vast Green Ocean of the Late 21st Century

once upon a yarn
this planet was full of trees
making oxygen

then lifetimes ago
man saw to their destruction
for fuel/production

sipping O_2 tanks
bankrupting their own offspring
man's greed could care less

this self-destruction
this ecological mess
this bleak disaster

this . . . is also true:
nature has corrective force
despite the abuse

cities now give way
whether or not they wanted
to trees upon trees

multiplying fast
suffocation all mankind
green oceans of trees

The Machine that Didn't Know

headed back to Mars
oceans on earth have dried out
revealing secrets

early ships still lay
stuck in ancient sandy beds
awaiting a crew

once upon boarding
activating all engines
so was its mission

translator running
minutes to find our language
then it spoke its truth

we, the descendants
a kinship among the stars
time that we returned

plotting coordinates
of course we know the planet
we've been there before

strong, windy deserts
its been dead long before man
how does it not know

As Old as Stars

⌐

twelve tet'rons ago
when this world was new to us
when the founders came

¬

we built great cities
with grand temples to our gods
per social contract

∟

we built crystal roads
from all this world had offered
wasting no resource

⌋

we built shopping malls
to remind us of home'world
what we left behind

⌐

we built everything
in the likeness of before
as our tradition

┐

now to this tet'tron
is all this place could handle
acts as old as stars

⌊

all Great Migrations
begin with much depletion
natural unrest

Space Man's Lament

⌐●

goodbye pretty whores
with your red skin and six breasts
with your long silk hair

┐ ●

with your supple lips
with your soft conforming hips
oh how I'll miss you

└●

goodbye pretty whores
who help me forget my life
out here in deep space

┘ ●

out here in the dark
out here in this vast nothing
out here so alone

⌐•
goodbye pretty whores
and all the great times we had
and all the filled space

┐ •
and all the great sex
and all the loudness that was
and all beyond this

└•
goodbye pretty whores
even if it was all lies
internal mirage

Citlaltemini

(brother from the stars)

●
I have seen blue skies
a beautiful place beyond
much further than home

●●
I have seen blue skies
where the bronze people worship
such as those like me

●●●
I have seen blue skies
with large constructed temples
lush delightful trees

●●●●
I have seen blue skies
discontent with simple life
long to stay behind

▬

I have seen blue skies
where soldiers can become gods
fulfill every lust

●
▬

I have seen blue skies
a concocted plan for three
against directives

● ●
▬

I have seen blue skies
soon they'll find out, here we'll die
. . . face up to blue skies

Coyolxāuhqui 3000

●

forgotten in time
where most ancient gods slumber
meters below stone

● ●

peace with centuries
preserved in countless pieces
they found her body

● ● ●

bronze prophet chanting
warns of not disturbing her
citing creation

● ● ● ●

sacrifice for gods
by the very gods themselves
men should not meddle

▬

white-science affair
fancies Frankenstein's folly
their will blinds their way

●

▬

modern miracle
stitched together and alive
the goddess reborn

●●

▬

gone now is the moon
as four hundred gods return
... we won't stand a chance

Mexico City, 2101 AD

●

priests of the night sky
awaiting for the return
upon pyramids

●●

slaughtering thousands
the best of all warriors
the highly esteemed

●●●

leaving no tribe out
taking no chances with luck
destined prophecy

●●●●

now moving forward
purging a conqueror's seed
born for this purpose

—

children of Cortez
massacred meal for mutants
fulfilling promise

•
—

old sky feels different
atmosphere bright-blue with change
a welcomed strangeness

••
—

spotted near Saturn
the feathered-serpent starship
Aztec god of old

Carnivorous Indigenous

(en el desierto mesoamericano de Chihuahua)

en ocotillo
far from pyramid builders
life owes much to death

a cave of scriptures
hides a historical truth
encrypted language

petroglyphs menus
paint a bloody obsession
of a time long gone

of light-skinned Norsemen
feasted by painted figures
with strange headdresses

one can estimate
for such an average lifetime
one could eat sixty

in these assumptions
body count is currency
highlights consumption

our past reminds us
in life, hunger has no friends
futures could be lies

The Visit

from a story I heard

Navajo Nation
during a dark time of drought
silence was a flood

one hot May morning
a woman who did not speak
spoke of a visit

at the door, they stood
tall strangers who came in peace
bearing a bad news

soon comes a dim light
people must be made aware
changes must be made

from death, no one hides
from danger, only few live
from warnings, a chance

they came to tell us
an indigenous future
deadly times coming

as they came, they left
leaving pollen and footprints
like none had seen since

Godzilla at the Pow Wow

drumbeat, drumbeat, drum
a deep rhythmic rumbling sound
music from the heart

he shows up sometimes
after messing up a place
to cool himself off

drumbeat, drumbeat, drum
back since the Astro-Monster
dancing for the win

dancing for his life
dancing for it is sacred
dancing for prayer

drumbeat, drumbeat, drum
he must be part NDN
puts him in a trance

pow wows aren't the same
without a kaiju stomp dance
peyote puff clouds

drumbeat, drumbeat, drum
reminds him of something gone
he never says what

the jettisoned

he had his moment
his sliver of history
to rule by his will

so, don't feel sorry
wasi'chu had it coming
it was prophesied

this is not by us
these troubling predictions
come from his own books

his master soon comes
from whom he says he learned from
yet, that's not his truth

things he did not do
were written that he comply
a life full of lies

he calls it rapture
pulling of the saints of earth
in the great judgment

fly to your master
fast from here with plenty speed
space is a desert

Red Eyes on Rockets

colonialism
those that came in peace did not
do they know our past

tall and majestic
as we were once thought to be
they were way much more

silky, olive skin
ten heads above our tallest
six powerful arms

oval, charming eyes
that held the secrets of time
embraced us as friends

it was us that came
wandering the cosmos
dropped upon their world

will they grow to hate
as we hated those that came
changed our way of life

earth's first nation-kind
we have discovered nothing
but peace in the stars

A Place Among Skies

ahtle

awake within stars
heaven is not a whimsy
home to living kin

ce

all across the skies
we find more Turtle Islands
filled with mighty tribes

ome

new generations
from old ones beyond this earth
stories we pass on

yei

seeding here and there
an ancestor instruction
as they did before

nahui

dance around the drum
like a dance from world to world
our Creator's plan

macuilli

learn to make rockets
migrate into the cosmos
ingrained DNA

chicuace

stagnate no longer
within wasi'chu's weak walls
built to trap your mind

Bury My Heart Under the Martian Sky

ages have passed by
or has it just been minutes
what does it matter

irrelevant time
at the end of a long line
all the clans are gone

at the beginning
we saw plentiful water
through the long-long glass

left, with plenty hope
a fresh world now drifting dirt
new ancestral lands

generations since
survival rates plummeted
I've buried them all

it took us too long
to finally get here from there
just to see us die

alone I remain
one voice, one near-silent drum
who will bury me

AUTHOR'S NOTE

What is a "haiku crown"?

That is usually the first question I get asked when I read and discuss these poems in public. I could easily end the discussion by saying that it's whatever I say it is, and that they should shut up about it already. That is what I want to do for sure, sometimes. But that usually ends up with fist-fighting, white-tenured English professors in university parking lots who say they know their "damned poetical forms" and damn if they are going to let some freakishly large, Indigenous Mexican-American rewrite their poetic curriculum standards. Maybe that happened once or three times too many. I could be lying . . . but the struggle is real. Or maybe I could get fake-book blocked by one or two independent poetry editors, a la keyboard warriors, who fancy themselves the greatest thing to happen to modern publishing, just because I call the enclosed pieces "haiku crowns" and I don't know what the hell I'm doing. Or that maybe I should go back to Mexico or whatever. Damn, pilgrim, you kiss your woman with that ugly mouth? But where would all that fun be without me?

    The great, grand, commercially-minded Google reminds me

that a "haiku crown" is a Hawaiian floral crown. Wait, that can't be right? I must have misspelled something. No, that's what Google AI is trying to tell me. Ok, fine. But that has nothing to do with poetic haiku. By the way, did you know that the word "haiku" was meant for both plural and single sets? Yeah, it was never "haikus" with an "s," professor. Anyhow, Google does go on and say that a proper "haiku crown" is "a poetic form that combines the traditional haiku structure with a thematic or stylistic twist, often used in competitions or creative writing exercises." Exactly what I am trying to say and do, except for the competition part.

I don't really have that in mind when I am creating a seven-set. Sometimes it's a smaller, three-haiku set like "Mexico City, 2101 AD," which first appeared in the Science Fiction & Fantasy Poetry Association's (SFPA) web-based *Eye To The Telescope: Indigenous Futurism*, Issue 41, July 2021. In addition, this set was numerated with the Nahuatl number system. This very poem in this very form eventually wound up winning a 2022 Dwarf Star Honorable Mention for poems of ten lines or less. This poem had ten lines online, technically. Only haiku numbers 1, 5, and 7 made up the original awardee, but today it is presented here with an expansion of four more haiku to make that magical number of a seven-haiku set or a "haiku crown." So also no, I don't have competition in mind when I write, and sometimes not even the length, mainly just the theme or thought of what I hope to convey.

As you see, my style of "haiku crown" creation/writing is very rudimentary and easy to follow. My form is simply a set or a string of seven haiku in the most basic American English haiku form, following the standard 5-7-5 syllable count. That's it: a group of seven haiku. Nothing fancy except for the subject matter. No mysterious poetic forms to be mishandled except for your intellectual biases. That's what some humans who have spent decades studying poetic forms and years getting complicated degrees, spend time arguing with me about, thinking that it gives "them" permission to berate me (and the rest of like-minded poets). You're getting red in the face again, professor. Drink some water. It's just my poetic style. Find your own.

What are "Indigenous Futurism" and "Chicano Futurismo"?

In my brown eyes and within my bronzed skin, they are one and the same. But let me explain even further. In an article soon to be published in the relaunched *Worlds of If Science Fiction Magazine*, I posed some questions where poetry could answer for another world where our existence, those of indigenous western hemisphere descent that is, was reversed or altered dramatically especially from the old colonizer policies and extreme politics of today which allow European immigrant descendants and their melanated, sellout sympathizers to round up any human being with a tint of brownness for monetary bounty and/or their racist self-gratification. History will not be nice to them if I can help it. Anyhow, I offered up the following possibilities:

> "What if the descendants of the Meshica successfully reached the surface of Mars before any modern nation and wrote a fresh creation story in their image? What if the Maya really came from 'out there'? And then returned to space after a short existence on Earth, only to crash land on the moon and eventually live inside what will soon be proven to be an ancient artificial satellite. What if the Apache developed the science of rocketry way before anyone else, and half of them had already left to live on better worlds? What if the Aztec Emperor Moctezuma II [my 16th great-grandpa, according to Ancestry.com, by the way] had ordered the exploration and subsequent conquest of what is to be Spain and eventually England and France? And then accidentally

introduced the Anglo-annihilating 'red pox,' wiping out millions in would-be Europe? What if John F. Kennedy had been born Diné and avoided the famous, public assassination at Dealey Plaza because of the advice of ancient, spiritual voices in his dreams? What if the Feathered Serpent Quetzalcoatl returned in a prophetic and boisterous, biblical-like Second Coming to destroy the enemies of his promised, bronze-skinned children? What if Abraham Lincoln's assassination was secretly carried out by the hands of a previously unknown Dakota Warrior Society instead of some desperate Confederate States' plot? What if putting together broken, ancient, Meso-American stone statutes brought fearsome, maize-people gods back to life to exact revenge on new, as well as old adversaries? What if modern, machine-gun-carrying Cherokee warriors traveled back in time to take out Andrew Jackson during the Creek War? What if the prophet Wovoka's Ghost Dance brought to life strong warrior wraiths with added uncanny supernatural powers to destroy the 7th Cavalry Regiment? What if Godzilla showed up to dance at pow wows and intermingle with the Plains People? What if the colonizing wasi'chu was only an indigenous boogeyman story that never materialized but only existed to scare children into bed? What if the Indigenous People of Turtle Island had a super-strong immigration policy to avoid the encroachment of all Europeans? What if? What if? What if?"

For some of these questions, I have already written responses. Some are even here in this very book. Of the other pieces and ideas, they remain floating still, collecting substance and truth developing within my heavily taxed, brown mind.

This thinking and writing, by people like me and others, is called "Indigenous Futurism." This is the approach of writing or speculating about a future in which we control the narrative, or a reverse world from the Indigenous point of view. The Indigenous peoples I reference here are those remaining whose ancestors once, and in some cases still, stretched from the most Northern point of the (now) Americas down to the most southern tip of it.

From here, regionally, I jump to adding the subcategory of "Chicano Futurismo." I am Indigenous primarily because my ancestors originated from central to slightly northern modern Mexico. By the way, according to more recent research, the ancestors of my ancestors quite possibly originated in Utah's "Place of the Seven Caves," also called "Chicomoztoc." So, there you go. Aztlan is literally pinpointed in the modern United States, according to yet another study. Furthermore, besides my indoctrination into and Indigenous practices of the Kiowa way, I am not currently registered to any US federally recognized tribe. But you well know, a politically forced border doesn't make me or millions upon millions like me any less Indigenous to this beautiful hemisphere. Otherwise, by this colonizer logic, the famous Native American Warrior, Geronimo, a Chiricahua Apache, is just another "dirty Mexican" since he was born in what is now a modern north-Mexican state, and therefore he cannot be a "genuine United States-born hero." What does your political border do to your thoughts now, ese?

So, a long history story made short, and in case you didn't know, the word "Chicano" comes from the original word "*Mejicano.*" "Chicano" was first used strongly by US citizens of Mexican descent during the civil rights struggle of the late 1960s into the 80s, and it stuck; and it even became "Xicano." For the most part, "Chicano" is a name Mexican Americans use to now denote their indigeneity and ancestral ties to the land and tribes that once was the whole of Mexico, especially at its expanse in the early 1800s (which now encompasses modern southwestern USA states).

Continuing according to sky-net (or whatever), "Indigenous Futurism is a movement in literature, visual art, comics, video games, and other media that expresses Indigenous perspectives of the future, past, and present in the context of science fiction and related sub-genres. Such perspectives may reflect Indigenous ways of knowing, oral history, historical or contemporary politics, and cultural perspectives." Sadly, the common list for influential Indigenous Futurist writers is short and includes the likes of Stephen Graham Jones (Blackfeet) and Darcie Little Badger (Lipan Apache). Did I ever mention that I was honored to share an "Indigenous Futurism Panel" with moderator and award-winning writer, Darcie Little Badger, author of *Elatsoe* (Levine Querido, 2020) and *A Snake Falls To Earth* (Levine Querido, 2021), at ArmadilloCon in Austin, Texas (August 22, 2022)?

Moving on into "Chicano Futurismo" within poetry, including myself, I count the likes of 2025 Horror Writers Association's Bram Stoker Award Winner and 2025 Elgin Award Winner, Pedro Iniguez, author of *Mexicans On The Moon* (*Space Cowboy Books*, 2024), as well as, Reyes Cárdenas, author of "Pachucos Y La Flying Saucer" (1975) and "From Aztlan to The Moons Of Mars: A Chicano Verse Novella" (2010) (both included as chapters in *Reyes Cárdenas: Chicano Poet, 1970-2010* by *Aztlan Libre Press*, 2013). Even still, there are a hundred or more writers writing prose than there are poetry in the field of "Chicano Futurismo," so I am not going to list them all except for one who seems to have earned a distinctive title to honor us all and that is Ernest Hogan, the "Father Of Chicano Science Fiction," author of *Cortez On Jupiter* (1990) and *High Aztec* (1992). I will also add that for a good look at this Chicano Futurismo "prose" writing field, you should look at these three related books containing plenty of these writers: *El Porvenir, ¡Ya!: Citlalzazanilli Mexdicatl* (*Somos En Escrito Literary Foundation Press*, 2022) a Chicano Science Fiction Anthology written primarily in English despite its title, and the same editors ensuing and similar projects, *Xicanxfuturism Codex I: Gritos for Tomorrow* (*Riot Of Roses Publishing Press*, 2025) and the forthcoming *Codex II* (2026) by the same California press.

Anyhow, still according to sky-net (or whatever), the topic, term, and form of "Indigenous Futurism" was coined in 2012 by Portland State University's Professor of Indigenous Nation Studies Program, Grace Dillon. Yet "Indigenous Futurism" and "Chicano Futurismo" didn't arrive by themselves. They were herald by yet another speculative genre: Afrofuturism. Afrofuturism is "a cultural aesthetic, philosophy of science, and history that explores the intersection of the African diaspora culture with science and technology" (according to sky-net, er . . . Wikipedia). Credit must be given where credit is due.

So overall, why bother to write in this genre at all? Well, for me it is to tell the story of the future (remember, there are no brown people in the Jetsons, just robot replacements with gray skin) or re-telling of a past we want to tell where the colonizer never came or met their demise at our hands. We must do it fast before the descendants of those same colonizers have a chance to write it for us. Look, they are already thinking they invented Mexican food (Taco Bell isn't real Mexican food) and probably Navajo frybread (it doesn't taste right from a can). They might even think that tomatoes (or *xitomatl*) and chocolate (or *xocolatl*) originated in Europe, too. So, don't wait till it's too late. Send all your money to the Indigenous people you know so we can correct this. Do it now! . . . Okay then, just tell your people about this book, pretty please.

What about this short collection of even shorter poetry?

So, let's talk about the actual subject matter in this book: the poems themselves. The first three poems are an exaggeration of the perpetual war between dogs and cats, and where that all might have originated, and how it might end. Do you know how it started? By the way, I'm a dog person, actually, but I did have cats in the past. I have the scars to prove it. Then I threw in my favorite, four-legged cryptids, *el chupacabras*, followed by the possible slimy origins of man. The next five poems are about the enduring tensions between humans and mermaloids. I speculate on the idea that man came from the sea, but in the end, will leave nothing to prove he once lived on this earth. The next five have to do with the folly of man's play with the occult and the limited helplessness of the mind. Then, it is on to three poems of man's messing with nature and how she responds back, and finally, it is off to the stars in a Heavy Metal Magazine kind of way. By the way, if you like Heavy Metal Magazine and experimental sonnets, I did such a thing in my 2021 Elgin Award nominated book, *Space In Pieces* (*House Of The Fighting Chupacabras Press*, 2020). But I digress. I then used the next several poems to imagine an Indigenous future, beginning with our origins, all the way to the bleakness or cheeriness of our possible end on other planets. As a nostalgic bonus, one of the poems does imagine Godzilla attending a pow wow to "smoke it up and chill" after "messing up a place." Godzilla is my spiritual kaiju.

Ultimately, this book of provocatively christened "haiku crowns," whose very mention makes English professors cringe as it pushes the sacred limits of their canonized poetic rules, incites you to your own creativity. Faced with plenty of discriminating obstacles (as well as a few poets and editors), and your idea of a good time, I hope this little tome delivers that expanding, speculative Indigenous/Chicano world I have tried to make you imagine. Like your first drink of mescal, your poetic taste will never be the same again, as I hope it brings you back for more. In the end, it was a good day to be creative. That is all I have to say.

Peace and Blessings to All My Relations. A-ho

ABOUT THE AUTHOR

Juan Manuel Pérez, a Mexican-American poet of Indigenous descent and the Poet Laureate for Corpus Christi, Texas (2019–2020), is the author of numerous poetry books including *Another Menudo Sunday* (2007), *O' Dark Heaven: A Response to Suzette Haden Elgin's Definition of Horror* (2009), *WUI: Written Under the Influence of Trinidad Sanchez, Jr.* (2011), *Live From La Pryor: The Poetry of Juan Manuel Pérez: A Zavala Country Native Son, Volume I* (2014), *Sex, Lies, and Chupacabras* (2015), *Space In Pieces* (2020), *Screw The Wall! And Other Brown People Poems* (2020), *Planet Of The Zombie Zonnets: Seasons One And Two* (2021), *Casual Haiku* (2022), *Christian Haiku For The Daily You* (2022), *Terror Of The Zombie Zonnets: Planet Of The Zombie Zonnets Season Three* (2022), *Live From La Pryor: The Poetry of Juan Manuel Pérez: A Zavala Country Native Son, Volume II: The Early Chapbooks* (2022), *Truth In The Time Of Chupacabras* (2022), and *Thirty*

Years Ago: Life And The First Gulf War (2023), as well as, the co-editor of the speculative poetry anthologies, *Unleash Your Inner Chupacabra* (2012; Archive Edition 2022) and *The Call Of The Chupacabra* (2018).

Space in Pieces, *Planet Of The Zombie Zonnets: Seasons One And Two*, and *Terror Of The Zombie Zonnets: Planet Of The Zombie Zonnets Season Three* were nominated for the Science Fiction and Fantasy Poetry Association Elgin Award.

Juan is also the 2021 Horror Authors Guild's Inaugural Lifetime Achievement Award winner and a 2021 Horror Writers Association Diversity Grant recipient. He is the 2011–2012 San Antonio Poets Association Poet Laureate, the Lone Star State's only El Chupacabras Poet Laureate (For Life), and a Zombie Texas Poet Of The Year. The former Gourd Dancer for the Memphis Tia Piah Big River Clan Warrior Society is also a Pushcart Prize Nominee as well as a SEATTAH Scholar (Striving For Excellence And Accountability In The Teaching Of Traditional American History) through the University of Dallas.

Juan is a ten-year Navy Corpsman/Combat Marine Medic (1987–1997) with experience in the 1991 Persian Gulf War (Operations Desert Shield, Desert Storm, and Desert Calm) attached to the 2nd Marines out of Camp Lejeune, North Carolina and was also a part of the 1992 Hurricane Andrew Relief Marine Air Group Task Force that went down to provide medical & linguistic support to a devastated Homestead, Florida.

This two-time Teacher of the Year, along with his wife, Malia (a three-time Teacher of the Year and now Librarian), is a co-founder of The House of the Fighting Chupacabras Press. Juan was also recently honored as one of the top ten 2023 Corpus Christi Hooks All-Star Educators in partnership with Reliant Energy, honoring exceptional teachers in the Coastal Bend.

The former migrant field worker, previously from La Pryor, Texas, currently worships his Creator, writes as well as conducts poetry and history workshops, and chases chupacabras in the Texas Coastal Bend Area.

To learn more about him, go to https://www.juanmperez.com/

ABOUT THE COVER ARTIST

Kolega Soberanis is a visual artist from Yucatan, Mexico. He began his career at the Centro Estatal de Bellas Artes in the area of Plastic Arts in Merida, Mexico. He studied Graphic Design and Visual Communication at university, and studied Digital Creativity with the international agency "Grupo W" in Coahuila, Mexico as part of an intensive semester. His work has appeared in magazines such as *Picnic Magazine, Chakota Mag, Kapix! Magazine,* and *Pinche Vida Zine,* and he has participated in books such as *Ediciones Invisibles, Sputnik,* and *Fundación Leer,* in Argentina.

Soberanis currently works independently as an illustrator for video game projects and editorial illustrations. You can find him at his portfolio and on Instagram:

Portfolio: https://www.behance.net/kolega_soberanis
Instagram: https://www.instagram.com/kolegasoberanis/

ACKNOWLEDGMENTS

A Place Among Skies first appeared in *Star*Line: Journal Of The Science Fiction And Fantasy Poetry Association, 46.1* (Winter 2023).

As Old as Stars appears here for the first time.

At the Temple of the Snake first appeared in *The Horror Zine* (Fall 2022).

Awoken first appeared in *The Horror Zine.com* (November 2021).

Bone Necklace first appeared in *Eye To The Telescope #42: The Sea* (October 2021).

Bury My Heart Under the Martian Sky first appeared in *Terror House Magazine* (October 4, 2022).

Carnivorous Indigenous appears here for the first time.

Citlaltemini first appeared in *Aphelion: The Webzine Of Science Fiction And Fantasy* (December 2022).

Coyolxāuhqui 3000 first appeared in *Aphelion: The Webzine Of Science Fiction And Fantasy* (February 2023).

El Monstro de Mejico/The Monster of Mexico first appeared in *Aphelion: The Webzine Of Science Fiction And Fantasy* (April 2023).

Godzilla at the Pow Wow first appeared in *British Fantasy Society* (2023).

Me by the Sea first appeared in *Hallowscream 2022: Gnashing Teeth Publishing* (October 31, 2022).

Mexico City, 2101 AD first appeared in *Eye To The Telescope #41: Indigenous Futurisms* (July 2021).

October Candy first appeared in *Terror House Magazine* (July 2, 2022).

Red-Eyes on Rockets appears here for the first time.

Space Man's Lament first appeared in *Aphelion: The Webzine Of Science Fiction And Fantasy* (April 2023).

The Devil in the Woods: He Speaks first appeared in *Strange World #2* (September 2021).

The Devil in the Woods: The Warning first appeared in *Strange World #2* (Summer 2021).

The Future Is Nigh appears here for the first time.

the jettisoned first appeared in *Star*Line: Journal Of The Science Fiction And Fantasy Poetry* Association, 46.1 (Winter 2023).

The Machine that Didn't Know first appeared in *The Horror Zine.com* (November 2021).

The Man Lost Between Forever and Ever first appeared in *The Horror Zine.com* (November 2021).

The Mermaloids' Lament first appeared in *Texas Poetry Assignment: #3 What It's Like Here Poems* (April 28, 2021).

The Other People first appeared in *The Horror Zine* (Summer 2023).

The Vast Green Ocean of the Late 21st Century first appeared in *The Horror Zine* (Summer 2023).

The Visit first appeared in *Eye To The Telescope #46: Quest* (October 2022).

This Blue World first appeared in *The Horror Zine* (Summer 2023).

What Dogs Know About Cats: Part I appears here for the first time.

What Dogs Know About Cats: Part II appears here for the first time.

What Dogs Know About Cats: Part III appears here for the first time.

INTERSTELLAR FLIGHT PRESS

Interstellar Flight Press is an indie speculative publishing house. We feature innovative works from the best new writers in science fiction and fantasy. In the words of Ursula K. Le Guin, we need "writers who can see alternatives to how we live now, can see through our fear-stricken society and its obsessive technologies to other ways of being, and even imagine real grounds for hope." Find us online at www.interstellarflightpress.com.

www.ingramcontent.com/pod-product-compliance
Lightning Source LLC
LaVergne TN
LVHW090039080526
838202LV00046B/3880